The Cancer Warrior

A Story of Courage

V.Madar Ramla Fathima

Ukiyoto Publishing

All global publishing rights are held by

Ukiyoto Publishing

Published in 2025

Content Copyright © V.Madar Ramla Fathima

ISBN 9789370094086

*All rights reserved.
No part of this publication may be reproduced,
transmitted, or stored in a retrieval system, in any
form by any means, electronic, mechanical,
photocopying, recording or otherwise, without the
prior permission of the publisher.*

The moral rights of the authors have been asserted.

*This is a work of fiction. Names, characters, businesses,
places, events, locales, and incidents are either the
products of the author's imagination or used in a
fictitious manner. Any resemblance to actual persons,
living or dead, or actual events is purely coincidental.*

*This book is sold subject to the condition that it shall
not by way of trade or otherwise, be lent, resold, hired
out or otherwise circulated, without the publisher's
prior consent, in any form of binding or cover other
than that in which it is published.*

www.ukiyoto.com

Dedication

I would like to thank my mother, Marjana Begum, and my father, Vajith Sahul Hameed, and my husband, Ibrahim, for their guidance and support throughout this fiction project. I'm also grateful to my family for their encouragement and patience.

Cancer Warrior
(A Story of Courage)

She comes home after her school,
and gives a form to her mom,
her eyes shining with excitement.
The form mentioned a talent exam,
her mom's face smiled and asked,
"You're just 14 years old,
and you're going to participate
in this talent exam?"
She smiles and says with confidence,
"Yes, Mummy, I will win this competition."

The Cancer Warrior

Her determination ignites
a fire within her,
as she prepares for her
competition with unwavering
focus and passion.
Mom wonders because
the form mentioned
the competition date
is three months later.

She took a book and started
studying for her talent exams,
immersing herself in the material
with enthusiasm.
Her dedication went beyond
just the exams,
as she also helped her mom
with various tasks.

She'd chop carrots and sweep

her room with care,
showing her mom that she was responsible
and thoughtful.
Her mom had big dreams for
her daughter's future,
and asked her what she
wanted to achieve in life.
"What do you want to be when you grow up?"
her mom asked,
curious about her daughter's aspirations.
The daughter thought for a moment
before responding,
"I want to be a doctor."

Her mom's eyes lit up with excitement,
and she asked her daughter to elaborate.
"I want to be a doctor
who truly cares about people,"
the daughter said,
"one who helps those in need."

"I want to provide free treatment to poor people,"
she continued,
"and make a positive impact on their lives."

Weeks go by, and she suffers
from a fever that can't be cured.
The mom rushes her to the hospital,
her heart filled with worry
and concern. She's treated,
and she happily comes back home,
but the joy is short-lived.

Days later, she again catches
a fever. The doctor informs
them to take a blood test.
Mom's heart sinks as she hears
the blood test result:
leukemia.
The parents hide it
from their children,
telling her she just has
a viral fever and needs
to be admitted to cure it.

The daughter fears going
to the hospital, but her mom
says, "You want to achieve more;
you must be healthy, my dear."
The daughter nods,
her eyes filled with trust
and determination.

The Cancer Warrior

In the hospital,
the nurse puts a drip
on her little hand,
and she cries loudly.
The next day, they inject her,
and she cries again.
The nurse unintentionally
tells the truth to the child,
"If you cry for just an injection,
how will we cure your cancer?"

The girl is shocked
and sees the room's title,
"Children's Cancer Ward."
But she doesn't tell her mom anything.
When her mom buys tablets
and comes to the room,
the child smiles at her,
a brave smile.

Weeks pass, and she doesn't

cry for injections, drips,
or even bone marrow tests.
The mom is stunned
because she didn't cry;
the mom wonders
how she became so strong.

The child asks her mom
to bring the competition
books to the hospital;
she wants to prepare for it.
Mom replies, "Child,
take a rest; after you're cured,
you can prepare for exams."
The child says, "I want
to win this competition,
and I also want to beat
this cancer." Mom is shattered
and asks, "Did you know
you have cancer?"

She smiles and says,
"Don't worry, Mom;
I will beat it."

Mom hugs her child
and says, "You're a strong girl,
my child; I'm so proud of you."
Months pass, and she prepares
very well for her competition.
Meanwhile, her cancer
gets worse; Mom comes

out of the room frequently
and cries secretly.

The girl doesn't cry,
even when her hair falls,
her appetite is gone,
and her hands shake.
The cancer tries
to make her fall,
but she stands,
and she stands even stronger.

The competition day arrives,
and the girl adamantly
goes to the competition.
The mom fears taking
her out of the hospital.
Finally, the girl completes
her competition.
Mom doesn't ask a single
word about the competition;
she just asks, "Are you okay, baby?"
The girl doesn't say
a word about her health;
she replies, "I did well
in my competition, Mom."

A few days pass,
and the girl is in ICU.
The doctor says to her mom,
"It's hard to cure her cancer."

The mom enters the room,
and the girl smiles at her mom.
But the mom cries
in front of her for the first time.
She replies, "Don't cry, Mom;
if you cry, it's considered
that the cancer won.
I'm happy, Mom;
I will never let
this cancer win."
Mom hugs her tightly
and says, "I love you, baby."
A few minutes later,
the doctors say, "Sorry, ma'am."
Mom is completely broken.

A call arrives:
"Is this Ramzana's mom?
She won this competition, ma'am."
The organizer says,"It's unbelievable

that a 14-year-old
won this national-level
competition."
Mom runs to her daughter's
side and says,
"You won, little child.
Maybe the cancer
takes your body,
but it can't take your soul;
it can't beat your thoughts.
You beat the cancer, my dear.

This is a true story about my sister,
a young girl with dreams
and aspirations.
She wants to live life
to the fullest,
to experience all the joys
and wonders it has to offer.

The Cancer Warrior

She dreams of becoming
a doctor,
of healing and helping others.
She wants to travel
and explore new places,
to meet new people
and make a difference.

But life has other plans,
and her journey has been
paused by cancer.
It's hard to understand
why this is happening,
why her life has been touched
by such a cruel disease.

In the hospital,
I've seen many children like her,
innocent and full of life,
yet struggling to survive.

A baby girl, just a week old,
with blood cancer,
a life so fragile and uncertain.

What did she do to deserve this fate?
What did my sister do?
They lived, they loved,
they were true to themselves,
but sometimes life is unfair and cruel.

In the hospital halls,
I've witnessed pain and suffering,
sisters losing siblings,
mothers losing children.
Many have lost their loved ones,
and the pain of cancer is a
heavy burden to bear.

Another story,
another warrior true,

The Cancer Warrior

Dr. Joyce, an oncologist,
shines through.
With compassion and care,
he heals the soul,
A good doctor,
with a heart that makes us whole.

He starts his rounds,
with gentle might,
An elderly man approaches,
with tears in sight.
"Thank you, doctor sir,"
he says with glee,

"My wife is better, thanks to you,
she's free to be."
Dr. Joyce smiles,
and reassures with ease,
"Don't worry, grandpa,
she'll soon dance with peace.
She'll laugh with delight,
and shine so bright,
Both of you will smile,
and cherish every night."

He visits Siddharth's room,
a little boy so dear,
Third-stage cancer,
but Dr. Joyce holds hope dear.
The parents lost faith,
but Dr. Joyce stands tall,
"I'll help him, don't worry,
he'll beat it all."

The Cancer Warrior

He gives the boy a chocolate,
and a smile so wide,
And holds his father's hand,
with a gentle pride.
"He'll be cured, don't lose your hope,
my friend,
We'll get through this, till the very end."

But when Dr. Joyce is alone,
in his room so still,
He opens a report,
with a personal chill.
A bone cancer diagnosis,
stage two so dire,
A warrior's own battle,
a heart that aspires.

He took treatment,
but can't give up his way,
His career is everything,

his passion each day.
He'll fight, he'll heal,
he'll shine so bright,
A warrior, a doctor,
with a heart full of light.

A few weeks passed,
and Joyce suffered with pain,
Severe leg pain,
a harsh reality to sustain.
He underwent an amputation,
a sacrifice so grand,
But his spirit remained unbroken,
his heart still in command.

He was confined to a wheelchair,
but his determination never waned,
People respected him more,
his courage unrestrained.
Despite the pain,

he continued to care,
For his patients, his passion,
his love to share.

Joyce successfully cured
Siddharth's cancer,
a miracle so true,
The boy said, "Doctor sir,
I want to be like you."
Joyce smiled and sent him off,
with a heart full of cheer,
A future doctor,
inspired by Dr. Joyce's dedication clear.

But fate had other plans,
a few days passed,
Joyce felt backbone pain,
his cancer's cruel grasp.
He was admitted to the ICU,
a week of uncertainty,

Later, news arrived,
his legacy, a finality.
A massive crowd gathered,
patients, friends, and family too,
To pay respects to Dr. Joyce,
a warrior, through and through.
His legacy lives on, a doctor, a hero true,
Dr. Joyce's story, a testament,
forever shining through.

Mohamed's story
unfolds like a thread
A young boy with a heart full of
life and energy
Football is his passion,
his escape, his joy
He'd run and kick and score,
without a care in the world

His father works hard every day,

to provide for his family
A laborer, with calloused hands
and a weary face
But Mohamed's smile is enough
to brighten up his day
A smile that says, "I'm happy,
I'm alive, I'm full of hope"

The Sundays are special,
the football matches a thrill
Mohamed waits eagerly,
his excitement building up
But fate has other plans,
and his life takes a drastic turn
He faints one Friday,
and his world is shaken

The hospital, the doctors,
the diagnosis
Cancer, a tumor,

a battle to be fought
The poor parents are devastated,
their hearts heavy with grief
But Mohamed, he's different,
he's a fighter, he's strong

He holds onto hope,
like a lifeline in the dark
His father's love, his football,
his determination to live
The football, a symbol of hope,
a gesture of love
A gift from his father,
with money he didn't have

The Cancer Warrior

Mohamed's eyes light up,
as he holds the ball tight
Tears streaming down his face,
as he asks if it's his own
"Yes, my dear," his father replies,
"you'll play again soon"
Mohamed's face lights up,
with a determination that's strong and true

"I'll play better than ever," he says,
with a spirit that's unbroken
"Because you bought me this football,
my own football, anew"
The weeks pass, and
Mohamed's condition worsens each day
But he remains strong, never giving up the fight,
in his own way

The doctors try their best,
to cure his cancer's might

But it's a battle, that's hard to win,
in the dark of night
Yet Mohamed remains brave,
a strong warrior, through and through
A testament to the human spirit,
that never gives up, anew

His story's one of courage,
of strength, of hope
A reminder that life is precious,
and every moment counts
Mohamed's legacy lives on,
a shining star in the night
A beacon of hope,
that guides us through the darkest of times

And though he may not win,
the battle against cancer's might
He's won something greater,
a place in our hearts, a memory that will ignite

A spark of hope, a flame of courage,
that will burn bright and true
A reminder of the human spirit,
that never gives up, anew.

A sixty-five-year-old Johncy
stumbled to walk.
She held her husband's hand,
always to walk.
He is the beginner of seventies,
but still he is the strength of Johncy.
He is the pillar of Johncy.

They have children,
but they are in abroad.
They talk to them through video calls,
that's enough.
The old couple helped each other
for all the time.
One day,
Johncy was faint
while taking money from the bank.
That day, this simple
old couple's life was shattered.

Yes, she also affected by cancer.
She has uterus cancer.
The doctor said, "She is old enough,
so it's very tough to treat her."
"Let her live her life for own."

John entered the room and asked Johncy,
"How is your health, baby?"

Johncy didn't tell about her life;
instead, she asked,
"I want to see my children."
John called his children
to tell this terrible news.
But they replied,
"Father, we can't come there,
but don't worry,
we will send the cost of hospital."

John replied,
"If you guys can't come to see your mom,
you don't want to send the money
for her treatment?"
John was getting angered and,
at the same time, very heartbroken.
Because she was in her last stage,
and she wanted to see her children.

John sold his nearby property

for Johncy's treatment.
But the doctor again said,
"It's not possible because she is getting old,
and it's very complicated."
John realized and decided to take Johncy
to her childhood dream island.
He booked tickets for that island,
but Johncy, without knowing anything.

The day arrived; the flight time was evening.
But that morning,
John awoke and saw Johncy's hand was in his chest,
but she doesn't hold her breath.
John hugged her and cried like a baby.

The children arrived,
from foreign lands so far,
Cried tears of sorrow,
at their mother's final star.
Guilt weighed heavy,

on their regretful hearts,
For not being there,
when she played her part.

Their father's anger,
a silence so profound,
A decision made,
to distance himself from their sound.
Their mother's last wish
, to see her children's face,
But they didn't think it serious,
in their busy, distant place.

Bablu's solitude echoes
parents lost in a car crash
twenty and shattered
left to face life alone

no warmth of family ties
no love to call his own

just emptiness and pain
until he finds a pup
lost and hungry, like him
he names it Popcorn

five years of companionship
laughter and tears
but fate's cruel hand
strikes again
cancer's shadow looms
Popcorn's numbness grows

Bablu's heart breaks
memories flood
of his parents' fateful day
tears fall like rain
but he wipes them dry
for Popcorn's sake

two years of struggle

medicine and pain
Popcorn's spirit weakens
Bablu's love remains
the doctor's words
a harsh reality
to let go, to end the pain

Bablu's decision
a mix of grief and love
to take Popcorn home
to find peace
a final goodbye

Popcorn's smile fades
but in death, finds peace
Bablu's heart still broken
finds purpose anew
a pet's organisation
to ease suffering
to fight for those

who can't fight alone

This cancer may have
taken many young lives,
Shattering dreams of teenagers,
and hopes of pregnant women,
and elderly souls
who fought in vain.

The fearless warriors,
brave and true,
Fighting cancer,
with hearts anew.
While others fear,
they face the test,
With courage bold,
they do their best.

Like soldiers in war,
they stand tall,

The Cancer Warrior

Unbroken,
with a spirit that enthralls.
The injections, tablets,
and radiation's might,
Can't shatter their will,
their hearts alight.

From freedom fighters to doctors, too,
Cricket players,
Olympians, and more, anew.
fathers, mothers,Sisters,
brothers, all fighting clear.

In hospitals,
day and night they stay,
Yet still they fight,
come what may.
Many have won,
beating cancer's might,
Their strength and courage,

a beacon bright.

Their stories inspire,
a testament to might,
A fight for life,
a shining light.
Let's honor their bravery,
their hearts of gold,
And stand with them,
as they battle bold.

It takes many lives,
but still, they face it boldly,
Fighting till the end,
their spirit unbroken.

A tribute to those who fight,
Living or dying,
their courage shines.

Though cancer may take
their body and strength,
Their will to fight remains,
A testament to human resilience.

Silent tears fall like
autumn rain
Relatives' hearts heavy
with worry and pain
Their loved one's suffering,
a weight they bear
Wanting to cure, to heal,
to make whole again

A mother's sleepless nights,
a father's quiet strife
Combing daughter's hair,
praying through the night
Hoping for a healthy life,
a future bright

Doctor, marriage,
babies, a life to live

But reality hits,
cancer's cruel grasp
Daughter's health worsens,
mother's heart does crack
Silent cries,
tears like a drying stream
A father's suffering,
hidden, unseen

The little brother,
unaware of cancer's name
Cries for his sibling,
feels the pain.

The husband broken,
wife's oxygen mask a sight
Wife's kisses on his hand,

The Cancer Warrior

love shining bright

Each relative a warrior,
unseen, unheard
Suffering, praying,
hoping, tears unblurred
Days and nights in hospitals,
a blur of pain
Irregular sleep,
medicine smells, trauma's stain

Their stories untold,
their hearts unspoken
The weight they carry,
the love they're broken
Yet they stand strong,
a fortress of love
For their loved ones,
they'd give anything above

Untold heroes, real warriors,
in every sense
Their love, their strength,
their hearts, their defense
For the ones they love,
they'd face any test
Their bond, their love,
forever etched in their chest.

Cancer's cruel whispers
echo through the night
Stealing life,
shattering hope, leaving scars
But what of the warriors
who stand tall?
Doctors who fight with
every fiber of their being

Their hearts beat with compassion,
their hands weave lifelines

The Cancer Warrior

Miracles born from dedication,
hope flickers
Even in darkness,
they refuse to yield
Ninety percent chance,
a slim thread, they cling to it

With every patient,
a new story unfolds
A life to save,
a future to shape
Doctors do miracles
with their treatment
Curing the incurable,
defying the odds

But what of the 10%
who slip away?
The doctors' hearts break,
their minds ask why

Why must innocence succumb
to this cruel fate?
Why can't we save them all?

The weight of loss,
the burden they bear
Yet still they rise,
unbroken, with hope to share
Their spirit unshaken,
their will unbroken
They seek answers,
push boundaries, and strive

To find a cure,
to end this suffering
To bring solace
to shattered lives
They make medicine,
try new ways
Even after failures,

they still have hope

A glimmer of
light in the darkness
A chance to heal,
to mend the broken
Their dedication,
a beacon of light
Guiding us through
the darkest night

One day,
a breakthrough will dawn
A cure will emerge,
cancer will falter
The doctors' unwavering spirit
Will bring solace
to shattered lives

Their fight is our beacon,

a testament to human resilience
Until that day,
they stand tall,
warriors against the tide
Refusing to yield,
refusing to lose
Their hope, their idea,
their technology

Will one day make a medicine
to cure this cruel disease
One day,
the world will be free from cancer's grasp
And the doctors who fought,
who never gave up
Will be the heroes,
their legacy forever etched.

In the realm of humanity,
they stand tall

Associations, trustees,
soldiers of compassion
Selfless hearts,
beating for others' sake
Their service,
a testament to love's pure make

Words fall short,
praise falters
Their dedication,
a shining star
Guiding lights in darkness,
hope's spark
For those afflicted,
they embark.

Across the globe,
they work tirelessly
Cancer associations,
trustees, angels mercifully

Treating the afflicted,
sheltering the poor
Creating awareness,
a world to explore

But amidst the genuine,
some masquerade
Fake associations,
money their motive's shade
Yet, the true warriors shine,
loyal and true
Their hearts,
a reflection of humanity anew

They seek out the homeless,
the lost, the alone
Cancer's victims,
and bring them back home
Innocent children,
saved by their care

The Cancer Warrior

Free cancer centers,
a haven to share

Unknown, unseen,
yet oh so grand
Real heroes,
transformed by love's command
God's embodiment,
in every form
Trustees, doctors, government,
centers, associates,
a symphony to transform

Their work,
a testament to humanity's best
A beacon of hope,
in the darkest nest
They toil, they strive,
they give, they care
Their legacy,

a world where love's always there

In hospitals, clinics,
and centers, they serve
A lifeline to those,
whose hope would swerve
Their compassion,
a balm to the soul
A reminder that love
makes us whole

Let us honor
these unsung heroes true
Their selflessness,
a reflection of love anew
May their work inspire,
may their hearts ignite
A world where cancer's pain,
becomes a distant light.

The Cancer Warrior

In today's world,
cancer's shadow looms large
A silent killer,
with many a change
Not a virus,
yet spreading fast
A result of choices,
that forever will last

Smoking's flames,
like a world fire spread
Teen boys inhaling,
a deadly habit's thread
Air pollution's toxic grip,
a constant threat
Industrial works,
chemicals, a hazardous feat

Food, a culprit,
in plastic's disguise

Easy to handle,
yet a toxic surprise
Frozen, instant,
a convenient lie
Innovation,
at the cost of health, we cry

Pregnant moms,
unaware, of the harm they bear
Instant foods, colorful,
yet toxic,
beyond compare
Children's chocolates,
colorful, yet poisonous too
A generation,
unaware, of the risks they imbue

Lifestyle's shift,
a sedentary plight
Smartphones, washing machines,

a physical inactivity's blight
No exercise, no movement,
a disease-prone fate
Cancer, a consequence,
of our modern state

Organic foods, a solution,
pure and true
Stop polluting,
our world, anew
Early detection,
a key to cure
Hospital visits,
at the first sign, we endure

Awareness, the shield,
that saves many lives
Symptoms, ignored,
a deadly stride
Fever, cough, lump,

a warning sign
Don't delay,
seek medical aid, in time

Let's spread awareness,
not cancer's fear
Educate, empower,
and take control, this year
Healthy choices,
a future to mold
Let's fight cancer,
with knowledge, bold.

Nurses, selfless souls,
by the bedside stay
Close to patients,
through every up and down day
They know the pain,
the fear, the tears
A constant presence,

through all the patient's fears

Twenty-four hours,
a watchful eye
A guardian angel,
who never says goodbye
They awaken,
like a mother's gentle care
Checking on patients,
with love and compassion rare

When a patient departs,
tears fall like rain
Not just relatives,
nurses and doctors feel the pain
The loss of life,
a weight they bear
A bond formed, a life lost,
a memory to share

Nurses, unsung heroes,
with hearts of gold
No task too menial,
no patient too old
They clean, they care,
they comfort and soothe
No disgust, just love,
in all they do

Respect to all,
who work in hospitals' halls
Cleaners, social workers,
standing tall
Each one a warrior,
in the fight against cancer's might
Their work,
a testament to humanity's light

Doctors, nurses, cleaners,
all on the same team

The Cancer Warrior

Fighting cancer,
a battle to redeem
Their work, a labor of love,
a sacrifice true
A tribute to humanity,
shining through

Let's honor these heroes,
who work behind the scenes
Their dedication,
a beacon of hope, a love supreme
For in the fight against cancer,
we all stand tall
Together, united,
we'll face it all.

About the Author

V.Madar Ramla Fathima

Madar Ramla Fathima is a 23-year-old emerging writer and recent MA English graduate. With a passion for storytelling and poetry, she has penned three short stories, over 10 poems, and a novel. Her novel ' The Magical Pendant ' is forthcoming with Ukiyoto Publishing. Fathima's writing often raises her voice on various issues, and her contributions have been featured in several journals. Her short story "Amaira - The Dream Warrior" achieved notable success, ranking number one out of 373 stories on the Wattpad application. With a keen interest in writing since her teens, Fathima continues to explore themes and ideas through her work. Her dedication to her craft and her unique voice have garnered attention, establishing her as a promising new voice in literature.

Fathima's writing reflects her creativity, passion, and commitment to storytelling.

www.ingramcontent.com/pod-product-compliance
Lightning Source LLC
LaVergne TN
LVHW041225080526
838199LV00083B/3364